Voyageurs

Also by Keira Andrews

Contemporary

Honeymoon for One
Beyond the Sea
Ends of the Earth
Arctic Fire
The Chimera Affair

Holiday
Only One Bed
Merry Cherry Christmas
The Christmas Deal
Santa Daddy
In Case of Emergency
Eight Nights in December
If Only in My Dreams
Where the Lovelight Gleams
Gay Romance Holiday Collection

Sports
Kiss and Cry
Reading the Signs
Cold War
The Next Competitor
Love Match
Synchronicity (free read!)

Gay Amish Romance Series
A Forbidden Rumspringa
A Clean Break
A Way Home
A Very English Christmas

Valor Duology
Valor on the Move
Test of Valor
Complete Valor Duology

Lifeguards of Barking Beach
Flash Rip
Swept Away (free read!)

Historical

Kidnapped by the Pirate
Semper Fi
The Station
Voyageurs (free read!)

Paranormal

Kick at the Darkness
Kick at the Darkness
Fight the Tide

Taste of Midnight (free read!)

Fantasy

Barbarian Duet
Wed to the Barbarian
The Barbarian's Vow

Voyageurs

BY KEIRA ANDREWS

Voyageurs
Written and published by Keira Andrews
Cover by Go On Write
Canoe Icon made by Freepik from www.flaticon.com is licensed
under CC BY 3.0

Copyright © 2017 by Keira Andrews
Print Edition

Second Edition. First published by Torquere Press in 2010.

ISBN: 978-1-988260-78-5

This is a work of fiction. Names, characters, businesses, places, events and incidents are either the products of the author's imagination or used in a fictitious manner. No persons, living or dead, were harmed by the writing of this book. Any resemblance to any actual persons, living or dead, or actual events is purely coincidental.

Chapter One

Montreal – 1793

A S ANOTHER BEAD of sweat dripped into his eye, Simon Cavendish swiped his forehead impatiently with his sleeve. "I'd heard it was cold in Canada." He'd had quite enough humidity in India.

The man behind the desk tried to hide his amusement. "It's still summer, Monsieur Cavendish. But do not worry, winter will be here very soon and you will not be complaining about the heat." He punctuated his statement with a laugh that shook his jowls.

Simon forced a smile and shifted in the wooden chair, wishing he hadn't dressed so formally. His waistcoat felt more like a corset, and he longed to remove his neck scarf and use it to mop his face. He'd kept his sandy hair short in India due to the heat, and it had become a habit—one he was very glad for considering the unexpected weather.

Shifting again, he resisted the urge to take his timepiece from the pocket in his breeches. Considering the fact that Simon himself was a month late, he supposed he shouldn't complain about his employer's tardiness.

The tapping of a walking stick signaled the approach of William Grant of the North West Company. The older man appeared and smiled politely. His white hair swept back from this forehead and round glasses perched on his nose. "Ah, Mr. Cavendish. We were afraid perhaps you'd decided to stay in England."

Simon stood and shook Grant's hand. "Not at all, sir. I'm afraid there was some dreadfully bad weather during the crossing and the ship needed repairs. The delays were interminable, but unavoidable. Now that I'm here I look forward to taking my post at Fort Charlotte."

"Hmm. Yes. Come into my office for a chat, won't you?"

After following Grant down a narrow hallway, Simon took a seat in the guest chair of the office. Leather-bound books lined the walls and a large map of the world hung on one of the walls. The window faced Vaudreuil Street.

"You come highly recommended from the East India Company. Experience dealing with the natives is very useful." Grant settled himself behind his large desk.

"Well, I'm not sure how similar the locals in India are to the Indians here, but—"

Grant waved his hand dismissively. "I imagine they're all the same for the most part."

"Well… Surely not." Simon had no idea what to expect of the natives, and he sincerely doubted they were interchangeable with those in India. He just hoped they were friendly.

"Tell me, why did you decide to come to Canada after India? You're what, twenty-seven? Wasn't there a nice girl back home in Surrey you wanted to marry?"

Simon flushed. *Not likely.* "I suppose I'm too much of an adventurer to settle down, Mr. Grant."

"Oh, this land is an adventure, I can tell you that." Grant chuckled. "Especially here in Lower Canada, where we are quite overrun by the French."

Simon laughed along, although he had never had much cause to dislike the French. He supposed being English was reason enough for most. "Well, I'm sure it will prove an adventure indeed. I'm eager to get started."

"Ah. This is where we run into trouble, Mr. Cavendish."

A queasy sensation unfurled in Simon's stomach. "Trouble?"

"I'm afraid all of our *voyageurs* are long gone on their way to Grand Portage and the fort."

"Voyageurs?"

"Yes, the travelers, as they're called. *Coureurs des bois* is another name for them—runners of the woods. Most leave in the spring, but we had scheduled a late trip to accommodate you and a clerk. However, when you were delayed, we had no choice but to send them without you."

The queasiness gave way to full-blown nausea. "Surely there must be some way?"

"It's a thousand miles via rivers and lakes. You were to go with one of our large boats—what we call a Montreal canoe. There would be ten men to help you on the journey and to do the paddling." He smiled ruefully. "We can't just call 'round another carriage as we would in England."

The nausea continued unabated and a rivulet of sweat dripped down Simon's spine. "Then what am I to do?"

"Wait until next spring. In the meantime we'll try to find some ways to keep you busy. You can learn more about the business and the culture."

Simon cringed at the thought. He came to Canada to explore and see the land, not to sit in an office in a city. "It's not even August. Surely we still have time."

"The journey takes six to eight weeks with a crew of eight or ten men. It's theoretically possible to make it before the ice, which comes to the interior usually in October, but—"

"Then I want to try. Please, sir. I came here to do

a job, and I'm determined to do it."

Grant sighed. "I appreciate your ardor, Simon. I do. But it's a dangerous journey at the best of times with a full crew. Even if I could rustle up a voyageur or two to accompany you—"

"But it's possible?" A quiver of hope flared in Simon's chest.

Grant regarded him for a few moments. "All right. Let me see what I can do. You must understand, though—you would be undertaking this trip at your own risk. If anything were to befall you, we would not be responsible."

Simon was already nodding. "Yes. Absolutely."

"Go back to your hotel and have a rest. I'll let you know as soon as I can."

"Thank you, sir." Simon jumped to his feet and stuck his hand out, pumping Grant's hand enthusiastically. "You won't regret it."

A RAP ON the door interrupted Simon's pacing. After months on a ship, he was used to making the most of small spaces, and his modest but clean hotel room didn't allow much freedom for wandering.

When he opened the door, he found a tall young man waiting in the hallway. "Hello!" Simon greeted him heartily.

The man nodded, unsmiling. "Mr. Grant sent

me." He said no more.

After a few awkward beats, Simon ushered him in. "Come in, come in. Sorry it's not very palatial."

The other man said nothing. He had shaggy, dark hair that fell over his forehead and he appeared to spend a fair amount of time in the sun. His eyes were a rather piercing green, Simon couldn't help but notice. He wore a simple cotton shirt and canvas pants, was fit and trim, and clearly spent a great deal of time doing manual labor. He looked barely out of his teens, if that.

Simon realized with a start that he was staring. "So what's the word?"

"I'm taking you to Grand Portage. We leave first thing tomorrow."

"Excellent! Good show. I'm sorry, I didn't get your name."

The man extended his hand. "Christian Smith."

Simon took Christian's hand, which was deeply calloused. "A pleasure to meet you. So you think we can make it in time?"

Christian shrugged. "You'll have to learn fast how to paddle. It'll just be the two of us."

"Not a problem at all. I look forward to getting out there. Have you been before?"

"Many times."

"Excellent. So Mr. Grant was able to convince you to make one more trip."

"He's paying five times as much."

"Ah." Simon wondered how much of the fee would be deducted from his own pay. Still, it was worth it.

"We probably won't make it."

"Oh! Goodness. Of course we'll make it." Simon smiled, but the nausea had made a bold and unexpected return.

Christian shrugged. "If we don't, they'll just send someone else next year in your place."

What a comforting thought. "Well, my trunk's still packed, so I'll be ready to push off tomorrow."

Christian gazed at the steamer trunk in the corner of the room. "You're not taking that."

"Is it a bit too heavy?"

Christian regarded him as if he were entirely the most idiotic man on the face of the earth. "Yes. We'll have packs we can carry on our backs."

"I hate to be a bother, but I need my things. I'll be overseeing operations at the fort, you see."

"It's going to be hard enough carrying the canoe."

"Surely the canoe goes in the water?" Simon laughed, trying to establish a rapport.

Christian didn't return his smile. "We'll need to portage across some parts of the land to get to the next river or lake, or to avoid white water."

"Sorry, I'm a tad confused. Portage? I know our final destination is Grand Portage and the fort, but…"

"It comes from the French. It means carrying the canoe. Over our heads."

Simon looked at his trunk, which had accompanied him all over India. He'd grown rather attached to it, as silly as it seemed. However, he had porters in India. It appeared Canada was a bit more on the rough side. "All right. You're the expert, after all."

"I'll bring you clothes and a pack tonight. I'll leave them outside your door."

"Oh, I have clothing. But thank you. I do appreciate the offer."

Christian looked Simon up and down. Suddenly Simon felt foolish in his breeches and stockings. He was glad he'd never caved to fashion and gotten into the habit of wearing powdered wigs.

"I'll bring you clothes." With that, Christian turned and left.

A few hours later when Simon returned from dinner with his new employers, the pack was leaning against his door. Several cotton shirts, canvas breeches and leggings were folded neatly inside. There was also what appeared to be a long, red woollen hat, scarf and mittens and a multi-hued fabric belt. A pair of surprisingly sturdy, tall leather slippers with beaded decoration sat beside the pack.

The sun was just peeking above the horizon the next morning when Christian knocked on his door. Simon had arranged with Mr. Grant to keep his trunk until it could be returned to him, and he'd packed as many as the essentials in the canvas pack as he could.

Christian picked up the bag. "Too heavy."

"I'll be able to carry it, don't worry."

Without asking permission, Christian knelt down an opened the pack so he could inspect the contents. The first things he discarded were three books. "They're only going to get wet."

Simon opened his mouth to object, but he supposed it was true enough. Still, he hated to be without Shakespeare and his cookbook from India. He'd had to remember the recipes as best he could and jot them down for the cook at Fort Charlotte.

Next, Christian pulled out several tins. "What are these?"

"My spices. From India."

"Are you going to trade them?"

The thought hadn't occurred. "No, they're mine." Christian opened one of the tins and peered closely at the orange powder. Simon told him, "That's turmeric. Excellent medicinal qualities and can be used to make some wonderful meat dishes."

"You should only bring essentials."

"My spices *are* essential. They're not heavy."

It seemed Christian couldn't argue this last point, and he carefully nestled them back into the pack. Simon sighed with relief. Not having his books over the winter would be bad enough—he wanted a few comforts.

Christian pulled out Simon's shaving kit. "Not essential."

"Why, Mr. Smith, I'm not a savage! I will need to keep up some modicum of civilized life."

Christian seemed suddenly incensed for a reason Simon couldn't imagine. After a moment he tossed the kit back into the pack. "Don't complain when you have to carry it."

Simon pulled at the collar of his shirt. The rough material scratched his skin and he felt as if he were a child playing dress-up. "Are you sure these shoes are appropriate for going into the wilderness?" The leather slippers were comfortable, but Simon would have preferred sturdy boots.

"Yes. Indians have worn moccasins for more years that you can count." Christian eyed him critically. "Where's the belt?"

"I don't think I need it. The pants stay up fine on their own."

"You need it. To hang your cup and pipe." Christian found the belt in the pack and handed it to Simon. As Christian waited, Simon fumbled. He wasn't sure what it was about Christian that unnerved him so. Simon was his elder and obviously his superior by rank and class. What did he have to be so nervous about?

Without a word, Christian took the belt from him and expertly looped it around his waist in seconds. He stood close, and Simon found himself holding his breath until Christian stepped back. They were a similar height, with Simon perhaps an inch taller.

Simon exhaled and smiled. "Are we ready to go on our grand adventure?"

Christian simply nodded and led the way.

Chapter Two

THEY WERE NEVER going to make it.

After a quick tutorial on the dock from Christian on how to properly paddle, Simon had carefully climbed into the front of the birch bark canoe. Christian steered from his position at the back, and periodically told Simon to paddle faster on one side or the other as he skilfully navigated the wide St. Lawrence River.

Now it had been three hours, and Simon's body ached already. His legs were cramped from kneeling and sitting on his feet. He pulled the paddle across his lap, and dunked his cup into the river. He could hear the quiet, rhythmic splashing of Christian's paddle dipping into the water. "When are we stopping for breakfast?" Simon ached all over and needed a break.

There was only silence, and finally Simon twisted around, causing his lower back to strongly protest. He grimaced, and Christian tossed him a cloth bag.

Simon opened it and found what looked to be dark, lumpy biscuits inside. "What's this?"

"Pemmican."

Simon took a bite, reminding himself of how he'd quickly grown to love Indian cooking when he arrived in Bombay. Besides, he was so hungry he'd eat just about anything. The pemmican was a dried, greasy kind of meat, with berries mixed in. Not the most delicious meal ever, but it did sate his hunger quickly. "What kind of meat is this?"

"Buffalo. From the west."

Christian pulled up his paddle and took a drink of water. Trees lined the banks of the river, and Simon could hear the sounds of nearby towns. Christian chewed on a piece of pemmican and Simon felt the need to make conversation, even though he was developing a kink in his neck from twisting around to look behind him. "How many hours a day will we paddle?"

"Fourteen."

A piece of the meat lodged itself in Simon's throat and he choked. After coughing, gulping down water, and coughing more, he was finally able to talk again. "*Fourteen*?"

"You want to make it to Grand Portage before the ice?"

"Well, yes. Of course. But—"

"Fourteen."

As if to punctuate his statement, Christian

plunged his paddle back into the river. Simon turned back to the front and picked up his own paddle, his arms crying out.

They were never going to make it.

As THE SUN rose in the sky and they left Montreal well behind them, Simon grew uncomfortably warm. There was a slight breeze on the water, but the non-stop paddling kept the sweat on his brow constantly replenished. He pulled up his sleeves and wiped his forehead when he could, taking short breaks.

Simon didn't know it was possible to hurt so much and still be conscious. His arms, shoulders and back ached from the repetitive motion of paddling. The paddle had been light enough at first, but had grown leaden as the hours ticked away.

They'd eaten a lunch of chalky biscuits, dried beans and more pemmican. Christian had lit his pipe after lunch and told Simon he should do the same.

"Oh, I don't smoke. It doesn't agree with my constitution, I'm afraid. I left the pipe you gave me in Montreal."

Christian shrugged and puffed on his pipe for a few minutes until he picked up his paddle. Then they were off again.

The sun was still far above the horizon when Christian angled the canoe toward the rocky shore.

Simon guessed it was about four o'clock, at least four hours short of the fourteen-hour mark. He could check his pocket watch, tucked safely in his pack, but it would require moving more than was absolutely necessary. As it was Simon could barely hold his paddle.

As they approached the shore, there was a sudden splash and Christian was in the water. He grabbed hold of the front end of the canoe, guiding it safely to a stop upon the rocks. Although Simon told himself sternly that it was time to stand up, his legs refused to cooperate.

Christian was clearly waiting for him to disembark, and with the last reserves of his energy, Simon hoisted himself up, holding onto each side of the canoe. He stepped out to the right and promptly tumbled face first into the water, his legs giving way.

Sputtering, he didn't resist as Christian's strong hands found his waist and hoisted him back up. Christian helped him over the rocks and sat him down on a boulder. Simon felt such a fool. "I just needed to cool off. It's rather warm today." He attempted a laugh.

Christian said nothing and hoisted their packs from the boat, carrying them a bit farther up the shore. He stood by Simon, waiting. "You have to help me lift the canoe."

"Are we finished for the day? I'll be ready for more in just a few minutes." Simon forced as much bravado into his tone as he could muster.

For the first time since they'd met, Christian smiled. "You did well. It's enough for today."

Flush with pleasure at the compliment, Simon wiped his face and stood. His steps were unsure, but he made it back to the canoe. Christian waded into the river once more to pick up the back end. On his signal, Simon strained with all his might and lifted the front of the boat a few inches. It was enough, and he propelled himself forward until the canoe was safely past the waterline.

Slumping down onto the hard sand, Simon stretched his sore arms. He laid back, the sun warm on his skin, drying his wet clothes already. Perhaps he'd just take a wee nap.

The delicious smell of cooking meat woke him. Wondering how Christian was able to start a fire so quickly, Simon opened his eyes and sat up with a start. The sun was almost beyond the horizon. Rubbing his face, Simon tried to shake off the doziness of sleep.

"Dinner's ready." Christian crouched by a fire ten feet away, stirring the contents of a small iron pot.

Simon couldn't believe so many hours had passed. "Why didn't you wake me? I could have helped with…that." Simon waved his hand to indicate the fire and pot.

"Sit." Christian nodded to a fallen log that he

must have dragged over to the fire. Simon was amazed he'd slept through it all. He did as he was told and Christian handed him a wooden spoon and plate. Christian carefully dished out the stew.

Simon blew gently on his dinner, eager to eat it but not wanting to burn his tongue. "What is it?"

"Salt pork and peas."

"Salt pork. That's the belly of the pig cured in salt, correct? Then soaked in water before being cooked. I ate it on board the ship. I was told it lasts a very long time without spoiling."

"Yes. We are *mangeurs de lard.*"

"I'm sorry, my French is a little…nonexistent."

"Pork eaters." Christian sat on the other end of the log and took a bite of stew, apparently unbothered by the heat. "That's what the *Hivernants* call us."

"The who?"

"The Winterers. Men of the North."

"And they are?" Simon was eager to learn about the voyageur culture. He took a bite of the meal, which was salty and fairly tasteless, but would certainly do under the circumstances.

Christian swallowed another mouthful and took his time answering. "They meet us in Grand Portage from the north and west, bringing furs from the back country. They return there for the winter, while we stay in Montreal."

"Ah, I see. Is there a rivalry between you?"

Christian shrugged. "They look down on us. Say we have it easy."

"Easy? If today was any indication, you certainly don't have it easy."

Christian washed down a mouthful of stew with a drink of water. "Today was easy. Other days will not be."

God help me, Simon thought. "Why did you become a…what was it? Pork eater? Why not be one of the northern men?"

There was silence as Simon waited for an answer, and he was about to apologize for prying when Christian said, "I wanted to see Montreal. Learn more of the world. I've seen plenty of the backwoods."

"I can understand that. Growing up in England, all I ever wanted was to escape." Simon waved his arm up at the sky, where stars were coming into sight. "To see the constellations from all the corners of the earth." He sighed contentedly, dinner warm and satisfying in his belly. "You really are a good chap for doing this. For taking me out to the fort."

"I need the money. It'll help me with my own travels."

"Yes, well. Still. I'm grateful."

Christian made a non-committal sort of grunt and then walked into the trees. A few moments later, Simon could hear him relieving himself. He realized he needed to do the same, but decided to wait a respectable time. He'd received a rather embarrassing lesson in the fundamentals of pissing over the side of a canoe early that day, and although he was sure he could handle going in the woods without instruction, he waited anyway.

Since the sky was clear, they slept under the stars that night, and Simon was amazed at how soundly he slumbered on the hard ground. He woke at dawn's first light to find Christian crouching at the water's edge.

His clothing lay on a nearby rock, and Christian's strong back muscles flexed as he splashed his face and chest with water. A bolt of desire shook Simon, and his morning hardness strained against his underclothing. Christian stood and Simon found himself unable to take his eyes from the other man's firm, round buttocks.

Simon had come to terms in India with his wicked desires, but had done little about them. He liked to believe that as a gentleman he was above these baser instincts. On the ship to Montreal, there had been an instance of late-night fumbling in a dark corner with a seaman, who had sucked Simon's cock with his mouth in the most delightful manner.

But otherwise, his experience with the flesh was limited to an unbearably awkward and unfortunate tumble with a parlor maid when he was a teen. He'd decided that he didn't really see what all the fuss was about.

Watching Christian's taut body in the faint light as night faded, Simon could better imagine the fuss. He longed to touch himself to relieve the building tension—no, he longed for *Christian* to touch him. At the thought, a gasp of breath escaped his lips.

Christian turned, and their eyes met. Simon quickly looked away, shamed. Although his muscles cried out, he stumbled to his feet and into the woods. He was still hard when he tried to piss, and he quickly brought himself off, biting his lip to stifle any sound.

When he returned to camp, Christian was dressed and ready to go. He said nothing as he waited for Simon to pack up. Simon's whole body ached, and the thought of getting back into the canoe was unpleasant in the extreme.

They pushed off before the sun was visible, Simon reminding himself with every torturous stroke that this was the adventure he'd wanted.

Chapter Three

SITTING ON A flat rock by the shore, Simon closed his eyes. He could fall asleep right there, listening to the birds chirping and the water gurgling. His muscles had become somewhat accustomed to the punishing schedule of paddling, but his entire body was still overcome with exhaustion at the end of the day. The endless hours of paddling, broken only by Christian's smoke breaks and a couple of quickly inhaled meals, had ground Simon down.

The insects were merciless in the interior, but as Simon rested, he didn't have the energy to swat them. On the days with no breeze, he and Christian covered their exposed skin with something called bear grease. It wasn't pleasant, but at least it worked and the insects only buzzed around and didn't bite.

The skies had remained mercifully clear in the week since leaving Montreal, and they'd been able to have a campfire each night. Christian had warned that it was a luxury they wouldn't always enjoy. As he rested, Simon could hear Christian rooting around in the nearby forest, collecting kindling. He could start a fire by rubbing wood together with an ease that Simon both envied and admired.

The sudden intrusion of an unfamiliar voice roused Simon from his stupor, and he sprang to his feet, wincing at the movement. Christian stood twenty yards away, facing four Indian men. Ignoring his sore limbs, Simon hurried to Christian's side.

The strangers didn't appear hostile, but Simon was keenly aware of the arrows and daggers they carried on their bodies, which were clad in loin cloths. The man Simon assumed was the leader spoke again, the words utterly unfamiliar to Simon. He looked to Christian. "Do you know what he's saying?"

Christian glanced at him, expression hard. "We don't all speak the same language."

"No, of course not. I just thought perhaps…" Simon trailed off, confused. *Who* didn't all speak the same language?

The Indian leader held up two dead rabbits by their oversized hind feet.

"He wants to trade," Christian said. He nodded to the man and walked over to his pack, pulling out a brightly colored scarf. It was light and shiny, although Simon could tell it wasn't real silk.

The Indians bent over the scarf, unfolding it and holding it up this way and that. With a nod, the leader handed Christian the rabbits. The Indians retreated into the dense forest and Christian and Simon were alone again.

Simon's mouth watered at the very thought of eating rabbit instead of the salt pork. He quickly went to his pack and pulled out his spices. "I'll cook if you'll make the fire." He felt a rush of invigoration.

Christian held out the rabbits. "Know how to skin them?"

The thought was decidedly unappetizing. "Uh, no. Not precisely."

"I'll teach you." Christian took out his knife.

Simon could hardly refuse the offer, and reminded himself that this was all part of the experience. After a lesson that resulted in fur and blood sticking under his fingernails most unpleasantly, Simon scrubbed his hands by the river as Christian started the fire. Christian had been a surprisingly patient instructor, which had pleased Simon in a strange way.

Simon cut up the rabbit meat and stirred it in the pot with some dried beans and his beloved spices. Although he could only guess from memory at the right combination and amounts, as he stirred in the turmeric the mixture took on the familiar orangey-yellow color of Indian curry that Simon missed so much. The smell was heavenly, and he breathed it in deeply.

When it was ready, he spooned the stew onto

their plates and sat back on the ground. Simon realized he was holding his breath as Christian took a bite. For some reason, he wanted to impress Christian. Wanted to please him.

Christian swallowed and was quiet for a moment. "You should cook more often."

"You like it?" Simon found himself grinning foolishly. He wasn't sure why Christian's opinion mattered so much.

Nodding, Christian took another mouthful. Simon tasted the stew himself and groaned with pleasure. "Oh, I've missed this."

"What do you call it?"

"We—the English, that is—call it curry. The Indians have many names for the different dishes, which are all delicious."

After a quiet minute of eating, Christian shrugged. "Can't compare to salt pork."

It took Simon a moment to realize he wasn't serious. "Was that a joke, Mr. Smith? I didn't think you had it in you."

Christian graced him with a rare smile, and Simon's stomach flip-flopped ridiculously. As they finished eating, he thought about what Christian had said earlier about not speaking the Indians' language, but he stayed quiet, not wanting to spoil the happy mood.

THEIR STREAK OF luck with the weather soon ended. Simon's muscles still throbbed with pain, but he'd gotten the hang of the paddling stroke and had just started to enjoy himself a tiny bit when the dark clouds rolled in.

He soon discovered that the only thing worse than paddling a canoe all day was paddling a canoe all day in the rain. They were farther inland now, and hadn't seen anyone else on the shore or water for two days.

"Should we stop until the rain lets up?" Simon had to shout to be heard above the deluge.

He was now accustomed to rather one-sided conversations with Christian, and didn't hear a response. Glancing over his shoulder, Simon looked for some sign that he'd been heard. Christian paddled as normal, fast and steady. He shook his head.

With a sigh, Simon turned front and dipped his paddle again. His clothes were already soaked, and without the sun, the air had turned surprisingly chilly. So far Canada had been almost as warm as India.

It was mid-afternoon when they reached the far end of a large lake they'd been paddling across for several hours. As Christian directed the canoe toward the hard sand beach, Simon chewed on a soggy piece of pemmican. He hoped to God they were stopping early after all. He was soaked and miserable.

At the shore he stumbled out of the canoe, his legs cramped and sore, as usual. He helped Christian drag the canoe out of the water and then collapsed, his breathing labored. Christian dropped down beside him and passed Simon his canteen. The rain continued to batter them and the wind whipped.

After only a few minutes of rest, Christian stood. "Time to go."

"What? Go where?" They'd reached the end of the lake.

Christian pointed toward the forest. "Portage."

Oh good lord. Simon had somehow forgotten about this aspect of the journey and the fact that the rivers and lakes weren't all connected. "In this weather?"

Christian didn't answer as he shouldered his pack. He stood by the canoe, waiting. Simon told himself to get up, but his body refused to listen. "How far is it?"

"Not far. Less than a mile."

"A *mile*? I should hope it is nearer than that indeed! How are we to be expected to carry the canoe that far?" He couldn't do it. It wasn't possible.

"Normally we'd each carry ninety pounds of trade goods as well as the canoe. Consider yourself lucky. Get up."

Simon bristled at the command. "Now see here, I don't take orders from…from…" He cast about for the right word but couldn't find it.

With a few strides, Christian stood directly in front of him, forcing Simon to look up. "From?"

"I'm your elder for a start." Simon got to his feet, and since they were of a height they were evenly matched. "You're barely more than a boy."

"I'm twenty. I'm a man." Christian's eyes blazed.

"A man who works for me."

"I work for the North West Company."

"Yes, and I'm to be in charge of Fort Charlotte, owned and operated by the very same North West Company. Clearly I outrank you, and I say we're staying here for the rest of the day."

Christian menacingly stepped closer, and Simon's heart rate doubled as a thrill of excitement whipped through him. "You knew what you were getting into. We have to portage. The canoe won't be any lighter tomorrow. If we don't keep moving, we won't make it before the ice."

"I don't care. I'm tired. I'm tired, and I'm wet and I won't go a step farther until I'm ready! You can't make me." Somewhere inside, Simon knew he was acting as a petulant child would, but he set his jaw stubbornly. He'd followed orders for weeks and paddled at a punishing pace. He would go no farther on this day.

Christian's gaze was steely. "I'm on this suicide expedition because of you. You will move when I tell you."

Simon's sneer was an imitation of his father's, a

man who had looked down on most everyone, including his wandering son. "I repeat, I do not take orders from the likes of *you*."

With a lightning-fast movement, Christian toppled Simon to the sand, his strong body holding him down, his forearm pressing on Simon's throat. "You may be a fine English gentleman, but out here, the filthy half-breed is in charge. I could leave you here. Let you fend for yourself. You wouldn't last a week."

Simon squirmed under Christian's weight, gasping for breath. Christian's body was strapping and powerful, and despite himself Simon was alive with exhilaration and desire. His body responded, much to his humiliation. With a muttered curse, Christian pushed off him and paced back and forth. Simon was utterly shamed by both his lust and his childish whining.

He sat up. "I'm sorry. I know we have to go on." Something Christian said finally registered. "What do you mean, half-breed?"

Christian's pacing ceased and his expression was unreadable. He said nothing.

Simon stared up at him, confused. "You said you were a half-breed. I thought you were English. Well, Canadian I suppose, but your name is Smith."

After a few moments of apparent disbelief, Christian laughed harshly. "You mean you can't tell?"

"No, obviously not." Simon belatedly realized that the tanned tinge to Christian's skin wasn't only from exposure to the sun. At Christian's dubious look, he added, "I'm not having you on. I didn't know."

"My mother was Ojibwe. An Indian." Christian clarified.

"And your father?"

"English."

"Where are you from?"

"By Lake Superior. My father was stationed at an outpost near my mother's village."

"Do your parents still live there?"

"No."

Simon realized Christian had spoke of his mother in the past tense. "Your mother is…"

"Dead."

Although this was clearly not a subject Christian relished, Simon found himself unable to stop talking. It was a nervous habit from childhood he'd never been able to break. "And your father?"

"In England."

"Really? Which part?" Simon shifted in the wet sand and realized the rain was finally letting up.

"Don't know."

"So you're not close then?"

"No." Christian opened his canteen and drank before refilling it in the lake.

"What's his name? Perhaps I've met him." Which was utterly ludicrous, but Simon didn't know what else to say.

Christian levelled him with a sardonic look. "John Smith."

"Ah. Rather a common name, I'm afraid. What does he do in England?"

Christian opened his pack and rummaged around. "Don't know."

"Was he here for long?"

"Long enough. Then he went back to his real wife. Real children."

"Oh. I'm afraid I don't quite understand."

"My mother was his 'country wife.' That's what the white men call them. He gave me his name and taught me English. Thought it would aid my heathen soul to call me 'Christian.'"

"Surely if he loved your mother he didn't think either of you a heathen."

"Love? She was practically his slave." Christian stood and swung his pack over his back. "Time to go." Clearly the conversation was over. Christian waited at the front of the canoe, his stare daring Simon to defy him.

Simon didn't argue this time and after putting on his pack, he went to the other end of the boat. On Christian's count, they rolled it over and then hefted it over their heads. Simon wavered under the weight, and the canoe was almost unbearably heavy on his blistered hands.

Christian led the way down a path through the trees. Simon followed, unable to see anything but

Christian's broad back and the underside of the canoe over their heads. Simon stumbled more than once on tree roots, and his arms and shoulders burned as he and Christian pushed onward. He concentrated on breathing and counting his steps. Anything to take his mind off the pain.

When Christian finally stopped, Simon staggered to his knees, the canoe crashing down on his head. He saw stars and groaned, rolling onto his back as Christian lifted the boat from him. Kneeling at Simon's side, Christian peered down. "Rest." He touched Simon's arm, and Simon felt a heat through his damp shirt where Christian's fingers splayed.

Then Christian was gone and setting up camp. When Simon was able to sit up, he realized they'd made it to the other side, and another lake lapped at the shore in the gloom of the late afternoon. It was a most welcome sight. They could still paddle for a few more hours, but Christian had clearly taken pity and Simon wasn't going to argue.

He was muddy with sand and dirt, and Simon stripped off his clothing and hurried into the water. It was cold, but he needed to feel clean again. Christian sat back on an outcropping of rocks, smoking his pipe, eyes closed. He'd taken off his shirt, and Simon admired the contours of Christian's chest. A surprising sprinkling of dark hark set off his silky-looking skin. Christian had the smooth, clean face of his Indian ancestors, and was amused whenever Simon pulled out his razor for a fastidious shave.

Simon backed up until he was standing in the lake up to his neck. He wondered what it would be like to touch Christian, and despite the chilly water, his cock sprang to attention. Christian's eyes remained closed as he puffed contentedly on his pipe. Simon took himself in hand while he had the chance, squeezing and stroking rapidly as he imagined touching Christian. Imagined tasting him.

Simon's breathing became shallower as he pleasured himself, watching Christian's lips close around the pipe, his long inhalations and the way he sighed as he breathed out. He thought about Christian on his knees as that anonymous sailor had been on the voyage to Canada. He envisioned Christian's mouth on him, his tongue dancing around Simon's cock. Simon's arm moved rapidly beneath the water, and as he came, he ducked beneath the surface to disguise his groan of bliss.

When Simon emerged, Christian's eyes were open and focused on him. Christian stared for a long moment, and then took another puff.

THERE WOULD BE no fire that night, so they quickly ate a cold dinner. Simon couldn't wait to reach Grand Portage and have proper meals again. When he returned from relieving himself in the woods, he saw that Christian had pulled the canoe farther up the riverbank. One end of the overturned boat was perched on a low rock. Christian unrolled a large, oilskin tarp over it. He glanced over at Simon. "This will keep the rain off."

Simon's heart skipped a beat. "We're sleeping under there? Both of us?"

Christian's expression hardened. "I'm not sleeping out in the rain."

"Oh, no! I wasn't suggesting you should." Simon felt so flustered and dim-witted. "It just looks… small." He was always saying the wrong thing. The thought of sleeping next to Christian in such close quarters set his pulse racing. They'd slept under the stars until this point, with plenty of ground between them.

Christian grunted a response and disappeared into the forest. The rain had slackened a bit, but Simon was still eager to take cover. He crawled under the tarp and the canoe. Although the ground was sodden, it was a relief to be out of the elements.

A few minutes later, he heard Christian's approach. Simon couldn't see much under the shelter, and he tried to squeeze himself over to one side. Christian shimmied in beside him, and although Simon had been practicing a deep breathing technique he'd picked up in India, his body still reacted. Christian was mere inches away and it was as if Simon could feel the heat of Christian's body.

Simon took a ragged breath. Christian's voice was loud in their little shelter. "Are you ill?"

After clearing his throat, Simon replied, his voice shaky. "No, no. I'm fine. Thank you."

Christian rolled over, his broad back so close to Simon. If Simon shifted only a tiny bit, his shoulder would press into Christian. He wondered if Christian would move away. Soon Christian snored lightly, and Simon reminded himself that he needed to rest. He was exhausted, and yet sleep refused to come. He listened to the rain on the tarp and Christian's deep, steady breathing. *He could reach out so easily...*

Finally Simon turned and curled into a tight ball, away from temptation.

Chapter Four

THE DAYS PASSED in a rhythm of sameness. They woke at dawn, or sometimes before it, and headed out in the canoe to begin ceaseless hours of paddling. Simon had never been so fit in all his life, but he was weary. He longed for a proper bath, with soap and the luxuries he'd long taken for granted, even in India.

They occasionally met hunters or other travelers, and they were often French speakers. Christian conversed with them easily because of his years as a voyageur, and Simon always had the uncomfortable feeling that they were talking about him. *Laughing* at him.

Yet Christian didn't seem a mean-spirited sort, and Simon told himself he was being too paranoid. Christian, and what Christian thought of him, occupied the majority of Simon's thoughts as they paddled onward. Simon knew it was silly, but he wanted to prove himself to Christian. Earn his respect.

One cloudy afternoon, as they finished a quick lunch standing by the riverbank to stretch their legs, Simon asked if he could sit in the back of the canoe for a change. Truthfully, he wanted a chance to watch Christian uninterrupted and unnoticed.

"You don't know how to steer."

"Well, I'll never learn unless I try."

"Why would you need to learn?"

It was an excellent question. "I'll be living out here in the Canadian wilderness. I think it would be of great benefit to me down the line."

"You'll have people to paddle for you at the fort if you need to travel. That's how it works, remember? Plenty of Indians to serve you."

"Still, I—"

"No. Not today. Maybe another day." With that, Christian walked back to the canoe and it was time to go.

Simon sighed and joined him. They paddled on, not speaking. Simon wasn't sure why Christian seemed so cross with him, and he wasn't about to ask. As the afternoon waned, Christian wordlessly steered them to shore, much to Simon's relief.

Christian and Simon both stripped off their sweaty shirts after disembarking and tipped the canoe on its side. It had been an unbearably long day, and Simon sat on the hard ground for a rest. He watched as Christian pulled the tarp over the canoe, Simon's eyes flicking over Christian's muscles as he worked.

With a glance, Christian caught Simon staring, and his jaw tightened. "Enjoying yourself?"

Simon's face flushed and he felt uneasy. "I just want to have a rest."

"Oh, I know what you want." Christian's laugh was more of a snarl.

"I don't know what you mean." Simon felt suddenly light-headed. The undertone of Christian's words was all too clear.

"You English. You're all the same. Away from women for an hour and you're begging for it."

Simon puffed up, reflexively indignant. "I don't have the slightest idea what you're on about, sir."

Christian strode toward him, his long, powerful legs covering the ground quickly as he discarded his colored belt and untied his breeches. "I'll show you, then."

Simon hadn't processed Christian's words before he was yanked around roughly onto his hands and knees. His cry of protest died in his throat as his trousers pooled around his knees and the cool air sent gooseflesh over his buttocks. Excitement ricocheted in his veins and he took a ragged breath as Christian reached for the bear grease in his pack.

As Christian's slick fingers found Simon's hole, Simon gasped at the sensation. Christian leaned over him, lips by his ear. "Beg."

Quivering with anticipation and need, Simon

warred within himself. No words would come to his lips. Christian repeated the command. "*Beg.*"

Simon's throat was dry as he rasped, "Please."

Christian's fingers gripped Simon's hips and he jerked him back roughly, thrusting into him at the same time. Pain exploded, and Simon cried out sharply. His arms and legs trembled and he held his breath. It was as if he was being torn asunder.

Christian froze in place, and after a few moments his grip relaxed on Simon's hips. One hand rose to caress Simon's spine, and then Christian's fingers wove through Simon's hair, suddenly tender. Christian slowly withdrew, and then inched back inside Simon with patience.

"It's all right," he murmured. "That's it."

His other hand reached around and took hold of Simon's cock, which had gone soft after the burst of incredible pain. Simon concentrated on breathing in and out steadily as Christian squeezed and rubbed him, bringing him back to life.

Pleasure joined the hurt, and soon overtook it, coursing through Simon's weary body. Christian stroked Simon with his hand and with his cock, moving deeper and deeper inside Simon until he reached a place that made the pleasure turn white hot. Simon moaned as Christian found the same spot inside him over and over and pulled Simon's cock harder.

Without warning, Simon was overcome, his body

shuddering as his climax swept over him. He collapsed onto his elbows, spent. With a few short thrusts, Christian joined him over the edge, and Simon felt the warm rush of Christian's seed spill inside him.

Gently, Christian withdrew. Simon curled onto his side, struggling to catch his breath. Christian was close behind him, his hand caressing Simon's hip. "You've never done that before." It was a simple statement, not a question.

Simon had to clear his throat before answering. "No."

"I'm sorry I hurt you."

"You didn't. Well, you did, but then…you didn't." Simon stumbled over the words.

Simon felt Christian move away, and a moment later one of the rough blankets lay over him. Christian said nothing else, and Simon could hear him preparing their evening meal. Simon's breeches were still tangled around his knees and he pulled them up.

He didn't know how to feel. Exhilarated. Embarrassed. Apprehensive. Excited. Confused.

Fulfilled.

They ate quietly as darkness fell. For once Simon had no idea what to say. They sat and dined as they did every other night, as if nothing out of the ordinary had taken place. *What does one say to the man who just buggered him?* At the very thought, arousal sparked, and Simon shifted uncomfortably on the hard earth, feeling the growing soreness in his rear end more keenly.

Rain began to fall as Simon washed their dishes, and he and Christian quickly gathered up their things and stowed their packs away under the tarp. They crawled under the shelter of the canoe as they had other nights, but now Simon was hyper aware of every sound and movement Christian made. Simon had longed for him before, but not like this.

Now that they'd been as one, the wanting had intensified to the point where Simon imagined his skin was crawling with it. He yearned to reach out and close the inches separating them in this dark cocoon. He yearned to hold Christian and be held.

It had finally happened. Simon Cavendish had lain with a man. Out in the open, in the waning daylight, for all the world—or at least the creatures of the forest—to see.

And he very much wanted to do it again.

CHRISTIAN, IT SEEMED, was utterly uninterested in coupling with Simon again. The next morning they rose as usual, and their routine was unchanged. Simon was in substantial pain, but he said nothing.

The hours sitting in the canoe did not help his arse, but Simon noted wryly that it took his mind off the ache in his arms and shoulders.

That night he watched Christian carefully from the corner of his eye, anxious for any sign that Christian might want to lie with him again. There were none.

Two days passed, and Simon resigned himself to the fact that his desire for Christian was clearly one-sided. After more endless paddling, paddling, paddling across a lake, they entered a narrow river with dense woods on either side.

The hot air was lank and still, and insects buzzed overhead. After maneuvering to shore, Christian and Simon stripped down and jumped into the water to cool themselves before applying the bear grease. Simon wondered, not for the first time, if the grease could attract actual bears, but he didn't think he wanted to know the answer.

It was only intended to be short dip, but they both lingered. Simon closed his eyes and floated, enjoying the respite. When he opened his eyes again, he was surprised and admittedly thrilled to find Christian watching him. Christian quickly glanced away and swam back to the nearby riverbank.

Simon followed, his eyes roving over Christian's bare body as they both left the river. Simon's own flesh rose, and he turned away to hide his excitement, memories replaying vividly in his mind. He heard a muttered word that sounded like a curse, and then Christian was close behind him, his hands catching

Simon's wrists.

No words were exchanged, and Simon eagerly went down onto his hands and knees. His bottom was still tender and sore, but he didn't care. He wanted it again. He wanted more. He wanted the pain and the pleasure.

But instead of Christian's fingers or cock, Simon felt a warm wetness. Gasping with the shock and the delightful sensation, he looked over his shoulder and saw Christian's head nuzzling him. Christian stroked Simon's thigh and urged him forward onto his stomach, sliding the rolled tarp beneath Simon's hips so his buttocks were raised.

Simon felt wanton and exposed, and that only heightened his exhilaration. Christian spread Simon's cheeks and his tongue returned to Simon's hole, soothing the sensitive flesh and creating great ripples of pleasure. Christian continued his licking and stroking, and Simon rubbed himself against the tarp, the rough material providing agonizingly delicious friction.

As Simon moaned his gratification, he marveled at Christian's act. He hadn't known people did such things, but now that he did, he couldn't wait to try it. He imagined what it would be like to taste Christian there, and he came, crying out. He struggled for breath.

They were both gritty with dirt, and the insects circled. Christian gave Simon a hand up and led him back into the water. Christian's hard cock bobbed before him and once they were in the river, Simon boldly reached for it. Standing close, Simon tugged and stroked as he would himself.

To his great relief and satisfaction, Christian closed his eyes and leaned into Simon's grasp, his lips open as he panted shallowly. After a minute, Christian shuddered and held himself steady with a hand on Simon's shoulder. Simon felt a ridiculous flush of pride that he'd been able to give Christian pleasure.

He wanted to draw Christian near and hold him. Their faces were mere inches apart, and Simon longed to feel Christian's lips beneath his. But the moment passed in a blink, and Christian was already wading back to shore. They dried off and applied the bear grease, saying nothing about what had just transpired.

Once back in the canoe, they paddled on as normal. Yet Simon found himself unable to wipe the smile from his face.

Chapter Five

FOR ANOTHER DAY, Simon and Christian once again acted as if they had never been lovers. Simon found it exceedingly torturous to pretend that he wasn't constantly filled with desire for Christian. He felt as if they were performing in some charade for a secret audience hidden among the leaves.

They encountered some French hunters midday who were happy to share some of their venison when Simon offered to make a curry. Although they wouldn't be paddling as much as they should for the day, it seemed neither Simon nor Christian could resist the lure of fresh meat.

The Frenchmen were a garrulous lot who kept up a constant stream of chatter as Simon prepared the stew with his dwindling store of turmeric and other spices. Christian nodded and said the odd thing, but Simon knew he'd rather not have to make conversation. Simon would have been delighted to, but of course couldn't speak the language.

After they ate, the men lingered, seemingly in no rush. Christian, however, stood and said a few words and then returned to the canoe. Simon packed up his supplies and followed Christian's lead, smiling and waving to the hunters as they pushed off from the riverbank.

They paddled on. "You don't like people very much, do you?" Simon felt pleasantly heavy and satisfied, his belly full.

"Some people. Not them."

"Why? They seemed a friendly lot."

"They talked of nothing but Indian women and their…uses."

"Oh. I see." Simon wondered if it made Christian think of his mother. He wondered, not for the first time, how she died. Perhaps he'd ask Christian one day, but it would not be today.

"The meat was good. I'll give them that."

Simon was happy to move onto a lighter topic of conversation. "Delicious! Are there many deer near the fort? I should like to have venison again."

"Yes. There are many." For some reason, Christian seemed not to want to talk about this either. Simon could sense the shift in his mood. He tried to think of something else to say, but came up empty.

They paddled later than usual due to their long and hearty lunch, and it was dark when they hauled the canoe ashore and set up camp. Christian soon sparked a campfire and they ate some of the salt pork.

When they finished, they washed down the salty aftertaste with a small flask of whiskey acquired from the Frenchmen. They hadn't brought any alcohol with them since Christian had insisted on packing as light as possible, so this was a rare treat.

Simon savored the burn of the liquor in his throat. It had been too long since he'd enjoyed a drink. He and Christian passed the flask back and forth, and they soon both loosened. Simon began telling stories he heard in India, regaling Christian with tales of palaces and princesses and the Hindu gods.

"And they lived happily ever after. Until this snake came along, that is. Nasty piece of work. But that's another story."

Christian's eyes shone in the firelight and a smile quirked his lips. *So beautiful,* Simon mused. Reaching out without thought, he tenderly cupped Christian's cheek. He wished they could stay like this forever. He was utterly fulfilled.

Christian froze, eyes wide, like the deer they'd surprised by the riverbank that morning. His skin was surprisingly soft beneath Simon's newly callused palm. Leaning in, Simon did what he'd wanted to do for weeks. As he brushed their lips together, Christian inhaled sharply. Simon retreated a few inches, and their eyes met.

Then all hesitation was lost as they came together, mouths opening, tongues stroking and exploring. As they kissed, a great sob of relief welled up in Simon's chest. *This* was what he wanted. *This* was what he needed. More than simply a sexual act. He needed *more*.

Falling back on the ground, flames of light licking their skin, Simon pressed Christian down, covering him as their kisses grew more frantic with need. With a few yanks, Simon wrestled off Christian's shirt and tasted Christian's chest, covering every inch with his mouth. He sucked Christian's nipples as his hand stole lower, following the trail of dark hair.

Reaching into Christian's breeches, Simon grasped him tightly and was rewarded with a loud moan. Simon shifted down and brought Christian's cock to his mouth. He hesitated, staring at the thick head in the firelight as the shaft pulsed in his hand. It was daunting, this new frontier.

Christian's fingers tangled lightly in Simon's hair. "You don't have to—"

Ignoring him, Simon took the plunge, swallowing Christian as far as he could. He choked and pulled back, coughing. Christian caressed Simon's hair, and catching his breath, Simon took the head inside his mouth again, moving slower this time.

The taste was oddly salty and musky, and Simon decided he liked it very much. He licked and sucked, tentatively delving further as Christian's moans increased, emboldening him.

With a sudden movement, Christian slid out of Simon's mouth and shimmied around on the ground, lying on his side. Before Simon could ask what was going on, Christian's head was in his crotch, his quick fingers opening Simon's breeches. As Christian's mouth enveloped him, Simon's breath was sharp with delight. Getting the idea, he returned his mouth to Christian's cock and did his best to mimic the movements Christian made with his tongue and lips.

Simon's senses were overwhelmed with taste and scent and unbearable pleasure. As Christian's tongue laved Simon's bollocks he shuddered and felt a rising tide within him. He dipped his head to do the same to Christian, nuzzling Christian's loins as the wave crashed over him. For a few moments he could only shake and moan, and then he returned to Christian, eager to give him the same pleasure. It wasn't long before Christian's warm seed splashed Simon's cheek.

The wind had picked up, and the fire sizzled as rain began to pelt down. Although Simon hated moving now that his limbs were heavy with satisfaction, they had to protect their gear.

When Simon wriggled under the canoe, he found Christian had put down a blanket, and in the darkness Christian's hands found him, peeling away Simon's newly wet clothing and then his own. Then they were skin on skin, bodies fitting together, hands and mouths discovering.

As the rain poured down outside their leaky cocoon, Simon kissed Christian, taking his tongue into his mouth and sucking on it. Christian whimpered in a way that sent blood straight to Simon's cock. In the cramped space, Simon couldn't get fucked the way he wanted, but Christian squeezed their cocks together, his fist tight as he rubbed and tugged, and Simon wasn't about to complain.

Christian's teeth found Simon's nipples and the little bolts of pain made Simon shudder and tingle. With another few breaths, the pleasure rushed over him as he cried out. Limp with exhaustion and fulfilment, Simon tried to finish Christian off, but Christian laughed and swatted his hand away as he quickly brought himself to completion.

Simon was utterly spent, and he was content to lie in Christian's arms as the rain tattooed its rhythm on the tarp overhead. They were both sticky and damp, but they inched closer, heads together. Simon had never felt so at peace, lying in Christian's arms, his breath warm on Simon's cheek. He was so full of…was this love? If it wasn't, Simon couldn't imagine what was.

After a serene interlude, Christian spoke first—a rarity. "You're like me, aren't you?"

Simon was puzzled. "Like you?"

"You wouldn't want a woman even if there was one here."

"No. I wouldn't." Simon was thrilled. Could Christian feel the same way he did? Did he sense the bond between them growing ever stronger?

"The others I've met, they…they weren't like us. For them it was just to fill a void. A need. Nothing more. They'd choose a woman if they could."

Simon pressed their lips together, wishing he could see Christian's eyes in the gloom. "I've never wanted a woman. And I want every part of you." It was a certainty that frightened Simon in its intensity.

"Even the parts that make me a man?"

Simon playfully traced the contours of Christian's cock with his fingertips. "Especially those parts."

Christian chuckled softly. "In my mother's culture, there are men who lie with men. Men who marry men. But they have the spirit of a woman and they live as women do. Dress as they do. Work as they do."

"This is accepted by the tribe?" He'd heard of something similar in India but had never witnessed it himself.

"Yes. There are also women who are men in their hearts. Fierce warriors, and they do battle as the men do. But I'm different. I'm a man, and I don't want to be a woman. Yet I want men. I don't fit there."

Simon was pleasantly surprised to hear Christian talk so much, and about his deepest feelings. "I don't quite fit in where I came from either. I suppose it's one of the reasons I love to travel. Although I don't fit in here. I'm not cut out to be a voyageur."

"Don't underestimate yourself. I didn't think you'd last more than two days, and look at you."

Laughing, Simon feigned offence. "Pardon me, sir? That was quite a dire prediction!"

Christian laughed along. "It's why I took the job. I thought I'd spend a couple of days paddling you down the St. Lawrence, and then you'd insist on turning around and returning to civilization. I demanded my wages up front, so I had nothing to lose. But you surprised me."

"Well, I'm sorry to have laid ruin to your finely crafted plans."

Fingers trailing up Simon's spine, Christian kissed him. "Don't be." He sighed. "I don't fit in your world, either. Maybe I'm better off out here."

Simon wriggled down, resting his head on Christian's chest. "You fit with me."

Christian's arms tightened around him, and Simon drifted to sleep, listening to the steady beating of Christian's heart.

WHEN THEY REACHED the near shore of the next lake, Simon couldn't believe his eyes. "Surely this must be an ocean?"

Christian had been quiet all day, but he smiled

now. "Feels like it when you're crossing."

They'd just finished another portage through the woods that took more out of Simon than he wanted to admit. He sat on the shore, eating a quick lunch. Christian seemed unaffected by the trek and examined a small gash in the side of the canoe. Simon stared out at the horizon, only an endless world of water visible. "Do we go across the middle?"

This garnered a guffaw from Christian. "Not unless you're seeking a watery grave."

Simon examined the lake. The water lapped at the sandy beach placidly, and the sun shone through a cluster of white, puffy clouds above. "Looks tame enough."

"Right now. You can't imagine how tall the waves can get. Even in the bigger canoe with more men, we follow the shoreline."

"Good lord, doesn't that take triple the time? At least?" Simon was exhausted at the very thought.

Christian chewed a piece of pemmican, his attention still on the canoe. He simply nodded.

"Surely with the weather this good we can take the risk?"

The only answer was a shake of Christian's head. Simon swallowed a handful of berries he'd picked the night before and tried not to think about how much of the journey still remained. He'd imagined once they'd reached this point they'd be almost there.

Yet as he stared at the endless expanse of water, a

deep dismay overcame him. He rubbed his stubbled face and sighed. He'd been too tired to shave the last few days. His ridiculous clothing were grimy with dirt and sweat and his moccasins never seemed to completely dry.

Too soon they were on their way, staying close to the shore as Christian insisted. When Christian began to sing a French song, Simon could barely believe his ears. Christian's voice was like one of the angels'. When the song finished, he turned over his shoulder. "Hidden talent, eh?"

Christian flushed and shrugged, but Simon could tell he was pleased. "Voyageurs sometimes sing to pass the time and keep in unison."

Simon turned back and resumed paddling. "It was lovely. Do sing another, won't you?"

Christian began a new song, and Simon closed his eyes as he paddled in time to the melody, listening to Christian's low, clear voice. He imagined being at the fort, sitting by a roaring fire with a nightcap in his hand and Christian by his side. Simon thought he would be most content.

Hours later as the sun set and Christian created a fire, he sang again, this time in the native language of his mother. Simon smiled to himself as he patted turmeric on a piece of salt pork. He was delighted Christian had become comfortable enough to share this part of himself. When the song finished Simon asked, "Do you know any carols? We shall have a concert at Christmas. I wager you'll be the finest singer at Fort Charlotte."

Christian poked the fire he'd sparked with a stick. He didn't look up. "Christmas?"

"Didn't your father tell you about it? It's a holiday we celebrate to—"

"I know what it is."

Simon brought the cooking pot over to the fire. "Oh. Are you shy about singing in public, then?"

Christian's expression was inscrutable. "No." He took the pot and placed in on a cooking rock in the fire. "Simon, I won't be there at Christmas."

"What? Of course you will." A strange panic flapped its wings in Simon's chest. *Of course Christian will be there.* "You can't make it back to Montreal in the winter. So you'll stay. With me."

"No. I'll go with the Winterers. Or to my village." Christian stood and went over to his pack. He poked through it, his lighter mood clearly vanished.

Simon's panic grew. "Why? Why wouldn't you stay with me? I thought we…" Simon motioned between them. "That we were…"

With a sigh, Christian stood and faced him. "What? Simon, there's no place for me there. What am I supposed to do while you're running the fort?"

Simon realized he hadn't considered it. "You'll…well, you can be…"

Christian's expression hardened. "Be what? Your *country wife*?" He spat the words.

"No! Of course not."

"Then what?"

Simon was at a loss for words. He had thought they were of the same mind; that they would naturally continue to be together. He admitted to himself that he hadn't considered the logistics, but it occurred to him with dawning horror and humiliation that perhaps Christian didn't share his feelings. Simon couldn't bear to imagine being without him after everything they'd shared, but for Christian, perhaps he had been but a diversion after all.

Christian spoke into the silence. "I've had enough of this place. After the winter, I'm going south. Maybe west. I want to see new lands. I'm my own man, Simon."

"I know that." Simon felt carved out. So many hours to think on this journey, and he'd only envisioned a dream of a future that couldn't be.

"You'll have everything you've wanted at the fort. But there's nothing there for me."

The words fell like blows and Simon turned away. With a deep breath, he nodded and escaped to the forest to collect himself, keeping his steps steady and sure. Christian's words rang in his ears.

Nothing for me there.

Not even Simon.

SIMON WOKE AT first light the next morning. He and Christian had eaten in utter silence the night before and stayed as far away from each other in their shelter under the canoe as they could.

But now he realized what had woken him as Christian's lips nuzzled his throat. His warmth surrounded Simon in the chill of the morning as he spooned up behind him. His voice was soft in Simon's ear.

"You know how the English are. You can't be commander and live with your half-breed boy. They won't allow it. We'd both be dead long before Christmas."

Simon accepted the truth in these words. In his joy at his newfound feelings for Christian, he'd closed off the part of his mind that was reserved for reason and rational thought. Even now, he wanted to protest. He wanted to insist that they'd find a way.

Christian continued. "This has been a dream. Soon we must wake."

Simon shifted around in Christian's arms to face him, and their lips met. They said nothing else, speaking instead with their bodies. They slid out from under the canoe and tarp, hands working quickly to remove their worn and grubby clothing. Christian spread the tarp and pressed Simon down onto it, their hands roaming as they kissed deeply.

As the sun inched above the horizon, they came together, Simon's legs draped over Christian's shoulders. Christian used the bear grease to open him, and Simon clamped down on Christian's fingers, his moans echoing across the vast water in the still morning. He urged Christian on, pulling his head down for another kiss as Christian filled him completely.

Pressing Simon's knees to his chest, Christian thrust into him, clutching Simon's hand, their foreheads together as sweat formed on their skin despite the morning frost. Simon swept his tongue into Christian's mouth, kissing him until they both gasped for breath as they rocked together.

As Christian hit just the right spot inside him, Simon cried out, his hard cock twitching where it was trapped between their bodies. Christian's arms trembled as he brought Simon to climax, hips like a piston. Simon clenched tightly, holding Christian inside him as deeply as he could.

With a shudder, Christian spilled his seed, gasping something that sounded like Simon's name as they kissed once more. They lay together, tenderly kissing faces, throats and chests as they held each other.

The sun was too high by the time they reluctantly roused themselves. They washed and dressed in silence, and shared a soft, lingering kiss before climbing into the canoe. As they paddled on, Christian sang a sweet melody that Simon couldn't understand.

Simon blinked away tears, glad that Christian couldn't see. He knew that although their journey was far from over, they'd already said goodbye.

Chapter Six

I N THE DAYS that followed as they traversed around the lake, a safe distance developed between Simon and Christian. There were no more angry words, simply a mutual separation. They paddled and ate, and Christian puffed on his pipe. He hadn't sung again since that morning.

They spoke civilly as they sat by the fire at nights eating another in the endless rations of salt pork. They still slept in close proximity beneath the canoe, but they did not touch. They did not kiss. No hands lingered on flesh, no lips caressed skin. Simon felt the loss keenly and hoped Christian did as well, although he couldn't tell if that was the case. Simon had never imagined he could experience a pain of the heart such as this. He finally understood the tortured poets he'd read in his school days.

The weather had turned decidedly away from summer, and the nights brought heavier frost and a bite to the air. The water, which had never been warm, became altogether too frigid for Simon to enjoy a leisurely evening bath. He shaved with water heated in the greasy pot.

Simon awoke the morning after they were back on a smaller river with a rough shake to his shoulder. He opened his eyes to find the sun already up, and Christian irritable and impatient. Simon tried to hurry, but his stiff limbs protested and Christian glowered as he was forced to wait. They shoved off under overcast skies, tension thick between them in the early morning air. Simon, feeling equally bad-tempered, grumbled to himself that Christian should have woken him earlier if he was so eager to get going.

After almost a full day of paddling, Simon heard a steady drone in the distance. He noticed the river moved quite swiftly, and he and Christian struggled to reach the shore. Simon heaved himself out of the boat, splashing through the cold water to pull the canoe onto the low rocks. His moccasins soaked once more, he grimaced as he stretched his legs.

He was well and truly tired of this voyage. At least he'd only had to battle boredom and cramped living space as he crossed the ocean. He'd never been so physically tested in his life as he had since coming to Canada. "What's that sound?"

"Rapids." Christian stood nearby, chewing on pemmican.

"Rapids? Is it safe?"

"We're walking around."

Oh, lord. Not another portage. Simon couldn't keep the groan from escaping his lips. "No. There must be another way."

Christian's jaw set. "There are two ways. In the water, or by land. We're portaging."

"How big are the rapids?"

"Big enough. Maybe if I had another voyageur who knew the water or was better with the paddle, we could do it."

Indignant, Simon straightened up. "After all these weeks of back-breaking work, I don't qualify? I think I'm jolly good with that paddle, thank you very much."

"Weeks?" Christian scoffed. "Weeks and months are nothing. You need years."

"I can do it." Simon was energized by a flush of righteous anger and a sudden and deep desire to prove Christian wrong. He'd show his worth, his measure as a man. Christian may not want him, not in the canoe or in his life, but Simon would prove he was as good as any other voyageur.

Christian shook his head emphatically. "You can't do it. Don't be a fool."

Simon was on his feet. "Yes, a fool. That's exactly what you think of me, isn't it? I'm just an English dandy, a buffoon. Just someone to trifle with and then discard like so much rubbish." Simon laughed bitterly. "I suppose I am a fool."

Christian's face softened. "Simon…"

Ignoring him, Simon stalked back to the boat, sending it back into the current with a mighty shove as he clambered in and picked up his paddle. *He could do this. He had to do this.* Christian splashed after him, barking his name. The current whisked them away from shore as Christian heaved himself into the back of the canoe, which came perilously close to tipping.

As Christian swore loudly, Simon paddled forward with determination, the din growing ever louder.

"Paddle when I tell you!" Christian shouted.

Adrenaline, resentment, and fury boiled in Simon's blood, and his pulse raced as the river swept them around a bend and the distant roar was suddenly frighteningly loud.

"Paddle left!"

Simon followed Christian's instructions as they narrowly missed a large rock. They were quickly approaching white water that churned furiously, and Simon understood with sudden clarity the mistake he'd made by giving in to his hurt and anger.

The spray of freezing water soaked him and his stomach lurched along with the canoe. They dipped and soared and suddenly rocks were everywhere in their path. A clammy fear seized him.

"Right! Paddle right!"

Paddling with all his might as they sped toward a

boulder, Simon clenched with terror, his heart in his throat. Oh, lord, he didn't want to die! They squeaked by and as he exhaled, the canoe dipped once more and a wall of water crashed over him. Simon clung to his paddle with one hand and the side of the canoe with the other as he sputtered.

They seemed powerless now to fight the current, which slammed them against a rock. As the canoe twisted, there was a strange lightness to it, and Simon thought they might be flying now.

He wrenched around, but it was too late. Behind him, the boat was horrifyingly empty.

"Christian!" Terror rocked him and he searched the churning water as he was swept ever onward. Another boulder loomed, and he paddled desperately, the canoe scraping by with a terrible sensation of being ripped open. Yet somehow he was still afloat, and the waters stilled now, the din receding as he came out the other side of the rapids.

"Christian!" Simon shouted his name again, praying for a miracle. Ahead, he saw a flash of something in the water, and he paddled frantically. It was Christian. Simon grabbed him by the collar, holding his head above water with one hand as he awkwardly attempted to maneuver them to shore.

Thankfully, the current pushed them toward the shore, and Simon was able to beach the canoe, heaving it upon the rocks. He leapt in the water, hauling Christian to safety. Simon laid him on the ground and looked anxiously for signs of life.

A cut marred Christian's temple, dripping blood down his cheek. Simon couldn't tell if he was still breathing, and he thumped on Christian's chest, panicked. Thumping again, he shouted Christian's name, his voice growing hoarse.

With a cough and splutter, Christian moaned softly. His eyelids fluttered and he coughed again, and Simon uttered a fervent prayer of thanks. He examined the rest of Christian's body for injuries and inhaled sharply over a sudden wave of nausea. His hand came away from Christian's left side covered in blood.

Grabbing a knife from his pack, still miraculously stowed in the bottom of the canoe, Simon gently cut away Christian's shirt. The nausea returned as he saw the full wound, a gash at least four inches long. Christian must have been dashed upon a rock after he was thrown from the canoe, and the guilt threatened to overwhelm Simon. It was his fault they'd gone down the rapids. If he hadn't been so stubborn, so prideful, it wouldn't have happened. Christian wouldn't be bleeding to death before his very eyes.

"No!" Simon's voice sounded foreign to his own ears. "No, I won't let you die."

Simon tore his own shirt off and bound it as tightly as he could around Christian's midsection to stop the bleeding. Christian was unconscious again, but he stirred when Simon pressed on the wound, whimpering in pain. Simon had never hated himself more in his life than he did at this moment.

The sun was making its descent, and night closed in. Simon bandaged the cut on Christian's temple as best he could with their meager supplies and kept pressure on the major wound on Christian's side. He needed to get help, but they hadn't seen a soul in days and he had no idea where they were.

Peering around at the seemingly endless and impenetrable forest, Simon gave in to his despair and cried bitterly. He couldn't carry Christian far, especially not without making the gash worse. It needed to be stitched, and he didn't have the tools, let alone the medical knowledge.

Come morning, he could try to get Christian in the canoe and paddle them…where? Christian was the navigator and they didn't even have a map. Christian didn't need one since he knew the way and the land.

His tears shamed him, and Simon forced himself to his feet to drag the canoe over to give shelter. He heaved it onto its side and positioned it over Christian where he lay motionless. He unfolded the tarp over the boat and wished he could provide Christian proper shelter. A bed, a fire, and blankets that weren't damp.

Careful not to jostle Christian too much, Simon slid under the canoe. He resumed the pressure on the wound and watched Christian carefully. He just wanted Christian to open his eyes and say that he would be okay.

Soon the temperature dropped and Christian began shivering uncontrollably. Simon inched closer and pulled Christian into his arms as gently as he could. They were both shirtless and he knew that skin-on-skin was the best way to share body heat. He thought of removing their breeches as well, but decided it would be too difficult in the confines of their shelter and with Christian's injury.

Simon prayed for morning and fell into a fitful sleep, nightmares running riot through his mind as Christian trembled in his arms. The night seemed everlasting, but just as Simon sensed dawn and light crept in, he heard voices.

It took him a moment to make sure it wasn't his imagination, or Christian muttering in his fevered sleep. Then footsteps neared, and before Simon could act, the canoe and tarp were lifted away. Simon peered up at three native men standing over him. One held Christian's blood-stained and ruined shirt.

Simon hoped these men were friends, and he allowed one to crouch down and examine Christian's wounds. When the man stood, he pointed at Simon and Christian and then toward the trees. "Come."

Chapter Seven

GRATEFUL FOR THIS divine intervention, Simon gathered the packs. Two of the men went into the woods and returned with thick fallen branches and fashioned a stretcher for Christian using the tarp. In the light of day, and now that he was paying attention, Simon could see that the canoe had been badly damaged on the rocks. Using hand gestures, the men indicated that they would return for the boat, and Simon nodded. He didn't care a damn about the boat—only Christian.

Simon quickly pulled on his spare shirt and followed the Indians through the woods. He carried his and Christian's packs since the men had insisted on carrying Christian themselves. Simon knew it was for the best, since he'd likely stumble on the unfamiliar path and injure Christian even further.

Oh, how he hated himself for what he'd done. He prayed once more that Christian would live and that they'd be granted a second chance.

The small Indian village was a collection of rounded, oval structures that Simon thought were called wigwams. He'd read a bit about Canada and its people on his journey across the Atlantic, and wished he'd used the time to learn even a few words of the Indians' language. Although he had no idea of which tribe these particular Indians were a part.

A buzz of chatter and activity greeted their arrival and Christian was taken inside a small wigwam covered in the same birch bark constructing their canoe. Simon had to bend to get through the door, and he knelt on the fur-lined floor, the thick hides making the wigwam surprisingly warm. Soon an older woman arrived, and Simon assumed she must be the healer. She examined Christian's wounds and he murmured and squirmed. The woman lifted Christian's head and forced a strange-smelling liquid down his throat.

Simon hated not knowing what she was giving him, but he knew he had no choice but to trust her. As she prepared to sew closed the gaping wound on Christian's side, she indicated to her two female helpers that they were to hold Christian down. Fighting his rising gorge, Simon stayed and watched.

As the needle pierced his flesh, Christian cried out and thrashed, fighting against the women gripping him. Sitting at Christian's head, Simon took hold of his shoulders and soothed him, telling him that it would soon be over. He wasn't sure if

Christian could hear him in his delirium.

It was torture to witness Christian in such pain, and Simon wished he could feel it in his stead. Finally the healer finished, and Simon caressed Christian's brow, alarmed at how feverish he had become. If only there was something he could do to help.

With a jolt, Simon remembered that he *did* have something that could help! The turmeric that he'd insisted on bringing on this ill-fated voyage was often used in India to fight infection on cuts and burns. Simon quickly dug into his pack and found the tin. He mimed to the women that he needed liquid and a container and one returned with water and a small wooden bowl.

Simon poured a portion of the turmeric into the bowl and moistened it until he could form it into a paste. The women peered curiously at the bright, orangey-yellow mixture and watched as Simon smoothed it onto both of Christian's wounds.

As the hours passed, Christian's fever seemed to worsen. The healer and her helpers came and went, but Simon refused to leave Christian's side. The women brought Simon food, but he couldn't bring himself to eat it, even though his stomach was completely empty.

Christian called out in his Native tongue, and the women soothed him in the same language. Simon asked, "Ojibwe?" and they nodded and said something he couldn't understand. All those hours in the canoe; he should have had Christian teach him a few basic words. He should have shown more interest in Christian's culture. He was an utter failure.

Simon reapplied the turmeric paste, but the fever raged on. Christian seemed not to know he was there, but at one point he heard his name among the string of foreign words. Simon's heart leapt. "I'm here, Christian. I'm here." He pressed a kiss to Christian's forehead, not caring what the women thought, although they appeared not to think anything of it at all.

The day passed and Simon remained at Christian's side, only leaving to answer the call of nature. Outside the wigwam, the villagers regarded him with open curiosity, but not hostility. He forced a smile for the children, despite his heavy heart.

Exhaustion eventually claimed him, pulling Simon down into oblivion despite his desire to stay awake and alert. He didn't know how long he had slept when he woke, blinking in confusion in the darkness, pushing a heavy fur from his body that someone had draped over him.

The village outside was silent, and inside the wigwam Simon only heard Christian's labored breathing. He wasn't sure what woke him, but then he heard his name. "Simon?" Christian's voice was a mere scratch of sound.

Simon was wide awake with a shot of adrenaline.

"I'm here." The moon overhead cast a diffuse light through the door of the wigwam and Simon could see Christian's face. His eyes were open, and he seemed alert for the first time since the accident. Simon caressed his cheek, thankful that the turmeric had done its job. "I'm here."

"Water." Christian struggled just to utter the word.

Scrambling to find the water container, he propped up Christian's head and helped him drink. Christian coughed violently, but still wanted more. When he was settled again, his voice was stronger. "Where are we?"

"An Ojibwe village. They helped us, thank the heavens. Oh, Christian, I'm so sorry. This is all my fault."

Christian tried to say something, but coughed instead. Simon gave him another sip. "Can you ever forgive me?" Simon held his breath.

After swallowing the water, Christian was able to speak. "Of course."

Simon exhaled, fighting tears. "I love you so much," he blurted. "I love you as I've never loved another."

Christian was silent for a long moment. "Si-mon…"

"It's all right. I know you don't feel the same. I just wanted to tell you. I couldn't live the rest of my life knowing that I hadn't. I'll always think of you,

Christian, no matter how many miles separate us." A weight Simon hadn't even known was there lifted from him.

Wincing, Christian reached up and put his finger to Simon's lips. "I didn't think I would ever feel love like this."

Simon's eyes filled with tears of joy and of sorrow. He kissed Christian softly as Christian drifted away, this time into a much-needed deep slumber now that the fever had retreated. Simon pulled the discarded fur over both of them and they slept.

IN THE EARLY morning, Simon awoke as the healer returned to check on Christian. She smiled at Simon and indicated the turmeric paste, nodding her approval at its effects. As the village stirred to life around them, the smell of cooking food wafted in and Simon's stomach grumbled loudly. The healer laughed, a welcome sound, and called out the door of the wigwam.

A few minutes later, one of her helpers appeared with a steaming bowl of something that resembled oatmeal. Simon was quite certain it was the most delicious thing he'd ever eaten. Then the girl brought a loaf of warm, freshly baked bread on a stick. Now *this* was most definitely the best thing Simon had ever eaten.

Christian stirred, and Simon smiled down at him, mouth full. Christian eyed the bread and returned the smile weakly. He tried to speak, but needed more water first. After he drank, he asked, "Enjoying your first taste of bannock?" Then Christian frowned slightly. "Your hands."

Simon realized his skin had been dyed the distinctive orangey-yellow by the turmeric paste. He hadn't even noticed. "The turmeric. I used it on your wound to fight the infection. Seems to have worked."

"Your beloved spices. It's a good thing you wouldn't leave them behind in Montreal."

"Yes, a good thing indeed. It might have saved your life." At the thought of losing Christian, Simon had to take a deep breath before the wave of emotion and fear passed. Christian shifted on his pallet of furs and flinched. Simon peered at him in concern. "Are you all right? Shall I fetch the healer?"

"No. I don't think I'll be moving for some time, though. It's good you have your spices. You might be able to trade them to a couple of the men here to take you the rest of the way."

"Rest of the way?"

"To the fort. There's only another couple of weeks to go if the weather holds."

"I'm not going to Grand Portage." Simon hadn't had time to even think about it consciously, but the words came so naturally. He knew it was what he truly wanted. The decision had already been made.

"What?" Christian's brow furrowed.

"I'm not going. I'm staying here with you."

"Simon, I could be laid up for weeks. The winter will be upon us soon, and the rivers will freeze. You have to go now. You can't wait for me."

"But I shall. I'll wait for you, and we'll spend the winter here, or in another village, or I don't know where. Somewhere. And when the spring comes, we'll go south, or west. Or east or north, even. It doesn't matter. We'll go wherever you want to go. I don't care what anyone thinks. We'll figure it out."

"Simon—"

"You said you wanted to see new lands. You were right, you know. We're the same, you and I. In so many ways."

"Your career. Your post with the company. You'd just abandon it?"

"Without another thought. I need never look back." Simon realized he was making an awfully big assumption with his bold ideas for their future. "That is, if you'll have me."

The smile that dawned on Christian's face was brighter than any Simon had seen before. "I'll have you, Simon. I'll have you."

Simon nestled beside him, and they kissed tenderly. Simon felt he might burst with happiness and affection. He wished they could truly lie together, that he could have Christian inside him again, completing him. At least for now while Christian healed they could make their plans.

Simon brushed their noses together, and they both laughed softly. "So where shall we go on our grand adventure?"

Christian kissed him once more. "Everywhere."

The End

Read breeches-ripping historical romance from Keira Andrews!

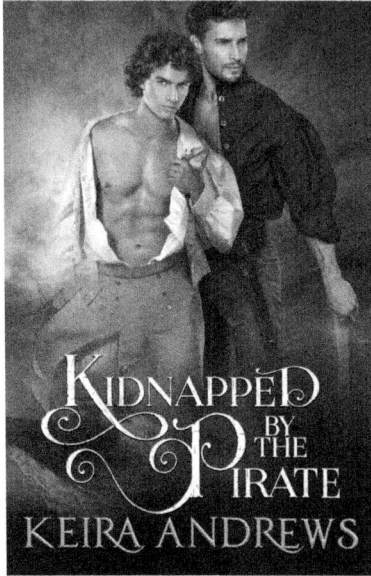

Will a virgin captive surrender to this pirate's sinful touch?

Nathaniel Bainbridge is used to hiding, whether it's concealing his struggles with reading or his forbidden desire for men. Under the thumb of his controlling father, he's sailing to the fledgling colony of Primrose Isle, where he'll surrender to a respectable marriage for his family's financial gain.

Until pirates strike and he's kidnapped for ransom by the Sea Hawk, a legendary villain of the New World.

Bitter and jaded, Hawk harbors futile dreams of leaving the sea for a quiet life. But men like him don't deserve peace. He has a score to settle with his captive's father—the very man whose treachery forced him into piracy—and he's sure Nathaniel is just as contemptible.

Yet as days pass in close quarters, Nathaniel's feisty spirit and alluring innocence beguile and bewitch. The desire to teach Nathaniel the pleasure men can share grows uncontrollable. What's the harm in satisfaction?

Hawk would never *feel* anything for him…

Nathaniel realizes the fearsome Sea Hawk's reputation is largely invented. He sees the lonely man beneath the myth, willingly surrendering to his captor body and soul. As a pirate's prisoner, he is finally free to be his true self. With danger mounting, the time for Hawk to relinquish his prize looms. Will his greatest battle be with his own heart?

Kidnapped by the Pirate by Keira Andrews is a breeches-ripping gay romance featuring a tough pirate too afraid to love, a plucky captive half his age, enemies to lovers, first times and exploration, and of course a happy ending.

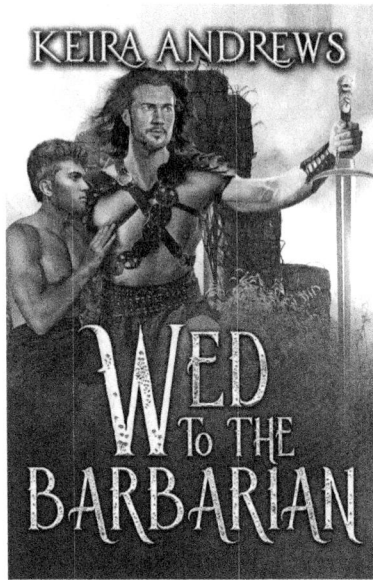

Will an innocent prince forced into marriage choose passion?

Sheltered in the palace with his books, Jem's life is peaceful. Even if he's lonely and yearning for romance, the big, strong men he wants don't crave small, timid princes.

Then he's forced to marry a mysterious barbarian.

Jem must do his duty—even if it means being stuck with Cador, a brute who dismisses him as weak. Even if it means a fake marriage in name only for the sake of their homelands. Even if he must leave behind everything and everyone to journey to a forbidding island of ice and stone.

Even if there's only one bed.

Alone with this wild—yet tender?—man, Jem discovers desire that burns hotter than he ever imagined. Can two strangers learn to trust, or will dangerous lies tear them apart?

Wed to the Barbarian by Keira Andrews is a gay romance fantasy featuring enemies to lovers, an age gap, forced proximity, first times, and of course a happy ending (eventually). This is the first action-adventure romance in the Barbarian Duet and must be read before *The Barbarian's Vow*.

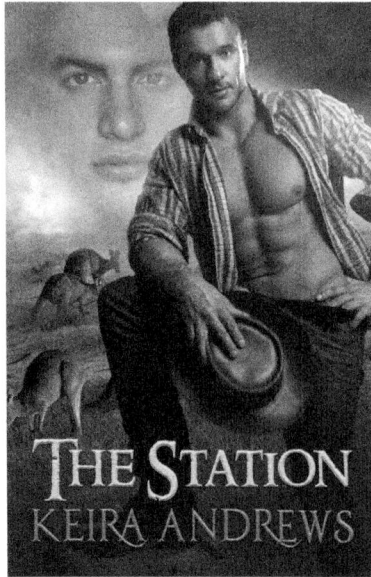

Two prisoners from different worlds find freedom and lose their hearts.

Ever since Cambridge-bound Colin Lancaster spied on stable master Patrick Callahan *mastering* another man, he's longed for Patrick to do the same to him. When Patrick is caught with his pants down and threatened with death for his crime, Colin speaks up in his defense and confesses his own sinful nature. They're soon banished to the faraway prison colony of Australia.

Patrick never asked for Colin's help, and now he's stuck with the pampered fool. While it's true that being transported to Australia is a far cry from the luxury Colin is accustomed to, he's determined to make the best of it and prove himself. Patrick learned long ago that love is a fairy tale, but he's inexorably drawn to sweet, optimistic Colin despite himself.

From the miserable depths of a prison ship to the vast, untamed Australian outback, Colin and Patrick must rely on each other. Danger lurks everywhere, and when they unexpectedly get the chance to escape to a new life as cowboys, they'll need each other more than ever.

The Station by Keira Andrews is a historical gay romance featuring an age difference, an eager virgin, hurt/comfort, and of course a happy ending.

A Note from Keira

Thank you so much for reading *Voyageurs*. I hope you enjoyed it! I'd be grateful if you could take a few minutes to leave a review where you bought this book, Goodreads, BookBub, social media, or wherever you like! Just a couple of sentences can really help other readers discover the book.

Thank you again for reading. Wishing you many happily ever afters!

Keira
<3

Join the free gay romance newsletter!

My newsletter will keep you up to date on my latest releases, news, and deals from the world of LGBTQ+ romance. You'll get access to exclusive giveaways, free reads, and much more. Go here to sign up: subscribepage.com/KAnewsletter

Here's where you can find me online:
Website
www.keiraandrews.com
Facebook
facebook.com/keira.andrews.author
Facebook Reader Group
facebook.com/groups/keiraandrewsromancereaders
Instagram
instagram.com/keiraandrewsauthor
Goodreads
goodreads.com/keiraandrews
Amazon Author Page
amazon.com/author/keiraandrews
Twitter
twitter.com/keiraandrews
BookBub
bookbub.com/authors/keira-andrews
TikTok
tiktok.com/@keiraandrewsauthor
Newsletter
subscribepage.com/KAnewsletter

About the Author

Keira aims for the perfect mix of character, plot, and heat in her M/M romances. She writes everything from swashbuckling pirates to heartwarming holiday escapism. Her fave tropes are enemies to lovers, age gaps, forced proximity, and passionate virgins. Although she loves delicious angst along the way, Keira guarantees happy endings!

Discover more at:
www.keiraandrews.com

Printed in Great Britain
by Amazon

55602594R00057